Three About THURSTON

BY
Susan Milord

Houghton Mifflin Company Boston 2005

One for my father

www.houghtonmifflinbooks.com

The text of this book is set in Berkeley Medium.
The illustrations are acrylic ink, watercolor, and colored pencil.

Library of Congress Cataloging-in-Publication Data
Milord, Susan.
Three about Thurston / by Susan Milord.
p. cm.
ISBN 0-618-42850-X
[1. Roosters—Fiction.] I. Title.
PZ7.M6445Th 2004   [Fic]—dc22   2003017726

ISBN 13: 978-0-618-42850-2

Printed in Singapore
TWP 10 9 8 7 6 5 4 3 2 1

Everything

Thurston had asked Roderick
and Mirabelle to join him for lunch.

He planned to make an enormous pot of soup.

He found a recipe for something called Everything-but-the-Kitchen-Sink Soup.

He gathered together all the ingredients and
carefully added them—one at a time—to the soup pot.

The soup was good, but it seemed to be lacking something.

"I wonder what it needs," Thurston said to himself.

Then he had an idea.

"There." He smiled. "That should do it."

"This is extraordinary soup," Mirabelle said.

"It's most unusual," Roderick agreed.

"What's in it, anyway?"

"Everything," Thurston began...

"...*including* the kitchen sink!"

Maybe,
Maybe Not

A crowd had gathered around Thurston.

"Who needs chickens?" he was saying in a loud voice.

"Sure, they're nice to look at, but they're just
smaller, weaker versions of roosters."

"Har, har!" the others laughed.

"Ask a chicken to carry a heavy box,
and she can hardly get it off the ground,"
Thurston said a little more loudly.
"Ho, ho!" the others roared.

"Race a chicken, and you'll leave her in the dust!"
Thurston practically shouted.
"Hup, hup!" the others hooted.

"Show me a chicken who says she
can do something, and I'll show you
a rooster who can do it better!"
Thurston declared at the top of his lungs.

"Your turn," Mirabelle said.

In the Cards

Roderick invited Thurston
over to his house to play cards.

A few minutes into the game,

it looked as though Roderick was winning.

Thurston made loud smacking noises with his mouth.

"Boy, am I thirsty," he said.

"Wait right here," Roderick said.
"I'll get us something to drink."

Several minutes later,
Roderick was still winning.
Thurston sniffed the air.
"Something's burning," he announced.

"I don't smell anything," Roderick said.

"I think you'd better check," Thurston insisted.

The game was almost over,
and Roderick was just about to win.
"I almost forgot!" Thurston exclaimed.
"I was supposed to meet Mirabelle for tea!"

He bolted out the door and down the street.

"I may not always win," Thurston said, "but I *never* lose!"